Books by Scott Corbett

The Trick Books

THE LEMONADE TRICK
THE MAILBOX TRICK
THE DISAPPEARING DOG TRICK
THE LIMERICK TRICK
THE BASEBALL TRICK
THE TURNABOUT TRICK
THE HAIRY HORROR TRICK

What Makes It Work?

WHAT MAKES A CAR GO?
WHAT MAKES TV WORK?
WHAT MAKES A LIGHT GO ON?
WHAT MAKES A PLANE FLY?

Suspense Stories

MIDSHIPMAN CRUISE
TREE HOUSE ISLAND
DEAD MAN'S LIGHT
CUTLASS ISLAND
DANGER POINT: THE WRECK OF THE BIRKENHEAD
ONE BY SEA
THE CASE OF THE GONE GOOSE
COP'S KID
THE CASE OF THE FUGITIVE FIREBUG

THE HAIRY HORROR TRICK

THE
HAIRY HORROR
TRICK

by SCOTT CORBETT

Illustrated by Paul Galdone

An Atlantic Monthly Press Book

LITTLE, BROWN AND COMPANY Boston · Toronto

LIBRARY OF CONGRESS CATALOG CARD NO. 70–77443

TR 04923 39 GI
LB 04746 32 F2

Seventh Printing

ATLANTIC–LITTLE, BROWN BOOKS
ARE PUBLISHED BY
LITTLE, BROWN AND COMPANY
IN ASSOCIATION WITH
THE ATLANTIC MONTHLY PRESS

BP

Published simultaneously in Canada
by Little, Brown & Company (Canada) Limited

PRINTED IN THE UNITED STATES OF AMERICA

To Geta Crowell

THE HAIRY HORROR TRICK

1

ALONE in their clubhouse, seated on boxes, Kerby Maxwell and Fenton Claypool were having a sinister conversation.

Kerby's face, which usually had a frank and open look, was filled with low cunning. Fenton's face, ordinarily as solemn as a public monument, was twisted by a fiendish grin.

It was just as well they were meeting privately in the small wooden shanty, out in the middle of the vacant lot beneath a solitary tree, with the door almost closed. If their parents had looked in on them then, they would scarcely have recognized them. If Mrs. Pembroke, Kerby's next-door neighbor, could have seen their expressions, her blood would have run cold.

They were planning the Perfect Crime.

They could not close the door tight, because then Fenton would not have had enough light to see the pad of paper he held on his knees. He barely had enough as it was. Outside, the fuzzy air of dusk in autumn was beginning to blur the outlines of fences and hedges and houses. A gusty breeze that sounded as if it were whispering evil secrets was harrying the last shriveled leaves off the lone tree and whirling them into a dance of

death. Scraps of gray clouds were scudding across a sullen sky, writhing like the ghosts of hanged men.

Fenton glanced out approvingly.

"It's going to be a perfect night for Halloween," he said, and began to draw on the pad.

"Well, I have to hand it to you, Fenton," said Kerby, "it's like you say, we're turning our disadvantages into advantages. If anyone had ever told me I'd be *glad* to have my cousin Gay on our hands tonight, I'd have said they were crazy. But now . . ."

Fenton nodded. "If Gay does her part right, we'll really fool Mrs. Pembroke this time."

Their plan of action was based on a close study of their victim's habits. Kerby and Fenton believed in the rule followed by so many successful generals: "Know your enemy." Mrs. Pembroke was their greatest local enemy. She made trouble for them every chance she got. She was a short, plump woman with a sharp tongue, a bad temper, and a big yellow cat named Xerxes.

Most of the trouble came about because of her cat. Just because Kerby's dog Waldo chased him once in a while, seldom more than two or three times a day, Mrs. Pembroke was sure that Xerxes was going to have a nervous breakdown. She could never get it through her head that Xerxes welcomed the chance to show off his tree-climbing ability. For that matter, it was about the only exercise he ever got, so that Kerby felt Mrs. Pembroke should have been grateful to Waldo, if anything. But grateful she definitely was not.

There was no possibility of peaceful coexistence with Mrs. Pembroke. When Halloween came along, then, the occasion always called for a little something extra in the way of hostilities.

This year's plan was based on Kerby's observation of enemy habits. Nearly any evening after dinner, if he cared to look, Kerby could go to the side windows of the living room and see Mrs. Pembroke over in her living room having her after-dinner nap in front of her television set, with Xerxes snoozing on her lap, while the evening newscast was on. Mrs. Pembroke called this "catching up on the news." She would never have admitted that she slept through most of it. Once Kerby had heard her say to a friend out on her front porch, "Every night after dinner I turn on the TV and catch up on the news."

Fenton held up the plan he had been sketching. It was a map showing Kerby's house and Mrs. Pembroke's house. It also showed the hedge between them, Kerby's driveway on the far side of his house, and the sidewalk and street out in front. In some ways the drawing looked like the diagram of a football play. It was full of X's and circles representing Gay and Kerby and Fenton, and dotted lines to show where each of them was to go at each stage of the plan.

6

"Now, then," said Fenton, "here's the way I see it. I'm at the telephone in your house, looking out the window. I have my flashlight ready. When we're sure Mrs. Pembroke and Xerxes are asleep, you sneak over to her back door. Gay goes to her front door. Gay is wearing her Halloween witch's costume and her mask. I dial Mrs. Pembroke's number. When I think the phone's about to ring, I give one quick blink with my flashlight. Right away, you and Gay poke the doorbells."

The picture of this synchronized attack brought on a fit of heartless chortling and snickering that lasted for some time.

"Everything starts ringing at once!" cried Kerby. "And if that doesn't make her shoot straight up in the air, and Xerxes with her, I don't know what will!"

"Then, about the time she comes down," said Fenton, "Gay jumps to the front window and raps on it and yells, 'Trick or treat!' And when Mrs. Pembroke sees a little girl, she won't know *what* to think. By the time she gets up and goes to the door, nobody will be there."

"She'll never suspect you and me," gloated Kerby. "She knows we wouldn't be caught dead running around with little girls on Halloween."

"And any other time, she'd be right."

"Right! It's a great plan, Fenton. I don't see how it can miss."

"Neither do I."

"And to think I was mad when Mom first told me Gay was coming over!"

Gay's parents were Kerby's Uncle Bob and Aunt Martha. Uncle Bob worked for the same company as Kerby's father. Both sets of parents had to go to a special company dinner that night. Gay had asked if she could stay with Kerby and go trick-or-treating with him. Kerby's mother had agreed.

At first Kerby had been furious. He had moaned and groaned and sulked, and declared his Halloween was being ruined. His mother had given him a lecture, all about how he should be *glad* he had a nice little cousin, which he found totally unconvincing. But then Fenton had come up with his plan, and that changed everything. Fenton was very good at such things.

A hard gust of wind whistled past and made the clubhouse door creak as if some nameless creature of the night were outside trying to get in. The eerie sound caused both of them to think of the same thing.

"I wonder what Mrs. Graymalkin is doing tonight?" said Fenton.

"I was just wondering myself," said Kerby. "Do you think she'll take her usual constitutional in the park?"

That was what Mrs. Graymalkin called her evening walk through Peterson Park, a small park not far from Kerby's house. Mrs. Graymalkin was the most interesting and unusual friend they had. Kerby had first met her in the park late one afternoon, just at dusk. She was a strange-looking old lady who wore a straggly hat with a long plume on it, and a draggly black cape over a draggly black dress, and high-heeled shoes that seemed strange and even daring for such an old lady to be teetering around on.

When Kerby met her, one of her high heels was caught in the drain near the drinking fountain. He helped her work it loose. The next afternoon, to show her gratitude, she brought him an old chemistry set that had once belonged to her little boy Felix. A Feats O'Magic Chemistry Set, it was called.

Since then she had told Kerby how to do some unusual tricks with it. Every time he did one, he had an amazing adventure.

All things considered, it had always seemed wisest not to let his parents know anything about Mrs. Graymalkin or the chemistry set. Kerby had a wooden chest in the basement full of old toys. He kept the set hidden in it under a lot of wooden blocks he had played with when he was little.

As the wind whistled again, Kerby enjoyed a shiver.

"Halloween ought to be a special night for Mrs. Graymalkin," he said.

Of course, a remark like that had its usual effect on Fenton. It brought his scientific look to his face.

"There you go again, Kerby, hinting around!"

9

"Well, you thought of her first."

"I did not. You said you were just thinking about her, too."

"But you said so first."

"Well, that doesn't mean —"

"Listen, you're not fooling me," said Kerby, pressing his advantage. "On a night like this, when it's Halloween, it's not hard to imagine that she might really be a —"

"Nonsense! Kerby, I tell you, there's no such thing as witches. I've told you so a hundred times, but you never seem to get the idea. Mrs. Graymalkin is odd. She's eccentric. She may even like to *pretend* she's a witch. But everything that's ever happened to us because of her can be explained by science."

"Ha! I'd like to see science come up with some of the tricks Mrs. Graymalkin has pulled off!" said Kerby loyally.

"Well, maybe she is a little ahead of her time," Fenton admitted, "but science will catch up with her someday."

It was an old argument between them. The subject had come up for discussion many times. But Kerby always enjoyed bringing it up, because his brainy friend always became quite worked up trying to defend science.

Fenton folded the map he had drawn, and put the pencil and pad of paper inside the box he was sitting on.

"I guess we're all set, Kerby."

"Okay, let's go back to my house. Aunt Martha and Gay will be showing up any minute now, and Gay will start yelling for us. Besides, I'm hungry, and Mom's going to fix special hamburgers the way we like them. That's because we're being so nice about Gay," Kerby added with a crafty grin.

When they had closed up the clubhouse for the night, they walked across the vacant lot to the fence that separated it from Kerby's back yard. They slipped through a place in the fence where a loose board could be swung to one side.

A car was sitting in the driveway.

"Hey, they're already here," said Kerby. "I'm surprised Gay didn't start yapping for us, or even come out to look for us."

"Maybe she didn't come over after all."

Light glowed from the kitchen window, throwing a warm yellow patch across the bleak outdoor gray. They could see Kerby's mother and aunt standing together at the stove. Light glowed, too, from the basement window beside the back porch.

"Someone left the basement light on, and it wasn't me this time," said Kerby virtuously. "Maybe Mom had to go down for something."

He paused to glance in through the window, and gasped. His eyeballs felt as if they were bouncing out on springs.

"Fenton! Look!"

Fenton looked, and his long, thin face grew sickly pale.

With Waldo sitting beside her, Cousin Gay was squatted down beside Kerby's toy chest, which was open. In front of her on the floor was a long wooden box, also open.

The box was Kerby's Feats O'Magic Chemistry Set.

2

KERBY reeled back from the terrible sight. So did Fenton. In fact, Fenton reeled back even farther, because he was taller.

If Gay let out one peep now, a whole chain reaction of troubles would be set off, and there was no telling where it would end. Kerby could imagine the kind of questions his mother would ask:

"Where did you get this? Who gave it to you?"

It would be hard enough to explain about the chemistry set, but how would he ever explain Mrs. Graymalkin? Parents would never understand someone like her.

"Fenton, what'll we do?"

"Listen, we've got to act natural. We've got to walk in and say hello, and ask where Gay is. When they tell us, we've got to walk over to the basement stairs, not hurrying, and go down and see her."

"Okay, we won't hurry — but we'd better be quick about it!"

Kerby had horrid visions of Gay rushing up the basement

steps carrying the chemistry set and piping in that high, clear voice of hers, "Look what I found!"

They opened the back door and walked in. Aunt Martha glanced over her shoulder at them.

"Hi, boys! Gay's in the basement," she told them, and turned back to say something about putting an egg in whatever she and his mother were making. Luckily they were very busy with their cooking.

When the boys reached the basement stairs, they shot down them with a rush that startled Gay. She was trying to jam the chemistry set back into the toy chest. When she saw who it was, however, she looked relieved.

"Oh, it's you! I was afraid it was Them."

Gay was a very little girl, small and dainty, the kind anyone would expect to bruise easily and be scared of everything. But instead, nothing ever seemed to bother her. She could take just about anything in her stride.

Kerby's voice was shrill with fury.

"Gay, what are you doing down here?"

"Not so loud, Kerby, we don't want Them to hear," warned Fenton in a low voice. He had remembered to pull the basement door shut, but even so it was a time for caution.

"I was only looking at your toys," said Gay. "Aunt Pris said I could."

She opened the chest and pointed.

15

"Where did you get that?"

"Never mind!"

"I didn't know you had a chemistry set."

"You didn't say anything about it to Them, did you?"

"No. The way you had it hidden under everything else, I knew it must be a secret."

"Well, it is, and don't you ever tell anyone about it, do you hear?"

"I won't . . ."

"Well, you'd better not!"

Gay gave him one of her brightest smiles.

"I won't . . ." she repeated, *"if* you'll do a Feats O' Magic trick for me!"

"What?"

"Well, gee, I want to see a trick!"

Kerby was rocked back on his heels by her ruthless demand.

"You mean you'll tell on me if I don't do a trick for you?"

"No! I mean I *won't* tell on you if you *do* do a trick for me," said Gay, as though there were a difference.

Kerby glared at his cousin. Girls! There was no limit to the depths girls would sink to in order to get their way. He closed the toy chest and sat down on it with a thump, arms folded, eyes blazing. Fenton jackknifed down onto a low stool. They stared at each other.

"This is blackmail!" complained Kerby.

"It is not!" said Gay. "I only want to make you do a trick."

"Well, what do you call that?"

As he sat there fuming, Kerby noticed Waldo for the first time. Waldo was prancing around with a big orange-and-black-striped ribbon tied in a bow around his neck. He was making an absolute fool of himself. Kerby pointed scornfully.

"Where did *that* come from?"

"The ribbon? I brought it to Waldo, special for Halloween. Doesn't he look cute?" said Gay, and Waldo nuzzled up to her with his pink tongue lolling out of the side of his mouth. He always acted like an idiot when Gay came over. The rest of the time, for the most part, he conducted himself like a self-respecting dog who was beginning to grow up and put puppy days behind him. But when Gay came over, this was the way he performed. He was very fond of her. He would let her get away with anything.

"Cute! Guh!" Kerby gagged disdainfully, and glanced at Fenton for support.

What he saw made him feel better.

Fenton was thinking.

Roosting on his stool like a stork, Fenton was thinking. The tall, thin boy's long face looked more solemn than ever, except around the eyes. Watching him, it seemed to Kerby that he could actually hear the wheels whirring at top speed as Fenton's finely tooled scientific brain went into action.

"If you don't get your way, then what?" Kerby asked Gay, to give Fenton time for more thinking.

"Well," said Gay, "then I'll have to tell Aunt Pris that you won't do a trick for me. Which I would *hate* to do."

Gay could be a devil, no two ways about that. And yet, he suspected she was bluffing. Because Gay never did things that were mean. The time she mailed some of his letters and got him into all sorts of trouble, for instance, she didn't do it to be mean. She thought she was helping him. And when it came to getting them back, she really was a help. After that business was all over, and they had told his parents all about it, Kerby remembered how his father tweaked her nose and said, "Gay, you're a born adventuress. I think you know instinctively the right thing to do in a pinch."

It was her record in this respect that had made Fenton and him decide to let her help play their trick on Mrs. Pembroke. Thinking about her now, Kerby was sure she was only bluffing. If she came right down to it, she would never tattle to his mother. She might be a girl, but she wasn't *that* kind of girl. What did worry him, though, was that she might slip up and say something without meaning to that would give everything away. Could Fenton think of a way to do something about that?

Without quite winking at him, Fenton stood up.

"Well, Kerby, I guess she's got us," he said. "We'll have

18

to do a magic trick for her. And if we're going to do that, we've got to see Mrs. Graymalkin first."

Kerby could hardly believe his ears. What was Fenton thinking of, mentioning Mrs. Graymalkin right out loud that way? Naturally Gay looked up at him excitedly and said, "Who's Mrs. Graymalkin?"

"She's a friend of ours," said Fenton, keeping his eyes steadily on Gay, and avoiding the stare of his thunderstruck friend. "She tells us how to do special tricks. Now, if you want to see a wonderful trick, you'll have to do exactly as we say."

"I will!"

"First of all, we won't be able to do it until after They leave," he went on, jerking his head in the direction of upstairs.

"Of course not," said Gay.

"Second, if we're going to do a trick for you we'll have to go right this minute and see our friend."

"Can I come, too?"

"No, you stay here, because we've got to run as fast as we can. They'll want us to eat supper soon. So you stay here. Waldo will keep you company."

"Well, all right, but don't be long."

"We won't be."

Fenton was already hurrying toward the stairs. Shaken to the core, Kerby tottered after him. Fenton, he feared, was slipping. The strain had been too much. Something had happened to that matchless brain. Only a mental breakdown, at the very least, would cause him to babble the way he had just been doing.

"I'll hide your magic set under your blocks again," said Gay.

"Okay," muttered Kerby. Anything to keep her busy.

When they reached the kitchen he was afraid his mother would say they couldn't leave.

"Mom, we've got to go outside for a minute! Gay knows all about it!" he said, and made a hopeful rush for the door.

"What? Oh. Well, don't be long. We'll be ready to feed you in just a few minutes now, and then we have to go. We're meeting your father and Uncle Bob at the hotel."

"I hope you don't mind having Gay around tonight," said Aunt Martha.

"Aw, that's okay," said Kerby, careful to keep his tone unenthusiastic and thus believable. Under the circumstances, it wasn't hard. "We'll be back in a minute."

As they escaped he heard his mother chuckle and say to Aunt Martha, "Halloween excitement . . ."

Halloween indeed!

At last they were outside and alone and he could go to work on Fenton as they ran down the street toward the park.

"Fenton, have you lost your marbles? Why did you tell Gay about Mrs. Graymalkin? I never heard such a —"

"Take it easy. I had to make it sound good, and get her excited, so she'd be willing to stay home and cooperate. Don't you worry. If we can just find Mrs. Graymalkin, everything will work out fine."

"How can things work out fine, if Gay knows about *her?*"

Fenton's eyes flicked his way.

"What if we can make her forget?"

Kerby almost stumbled over his own feet.

"Make her *forget?* How can we do that?"

"I've been reading a lot lately about something that science is using more and more. . . ."

"What?"

For an instant Fenton's solemn face broke into a wide smile.

"Hypnotism!"

This time Kerby did stumble, and all but took a spill.

"What? Hypnotism?"

"That's right. We're going to find out how to hypnotize Gay, and while she's hypnotized we'll command her to forget all about the chemistry set and magic tricks and Mrs. Graymalkin. What could be more scientific than that?"

22

3

IT TOOK half a block or so for Kerby to grasp the brilliance of Fenton's idea.

"Hypnotism! Are you sure it will work?"

"Yes. I've read a lot about it, and I'm sure it will — especially when we have Mrs. Graymalkin to help us."

"And it won't hurt Gay? I mean, it won't hurt her mind, or anything like that?"

"Certainly not. She'll simply obey an order to forget all about the chemistry set."

They had reached the corner across from the park. A welcome sight greeted them.

"Look!" cried Kerby. "There's Nostradamus!"

He pointed to a car parked across the street. It was an ancient sedan, tall and gaunt, with brass-rimmed headlights and flat fenders. The old car looked as if it would be lucky to make it to the nearest junkyard, but they knew from experience that when it came to performance, Nostradamus had what it took. That was what Mrs. Graymalkin called her old car: Nostradamus.

"We're in luck!" said Fenton. "She's in the park!"

Under the tall trees the fading light of day was dim and shadowy. The breeze that had been strong a short while ago had dropped off, so that now the few autumn leaves not yet ripped from the branches were scarcely stirring. The air was damp and clammy. A deep quiet reigned among the trees.

The boys sprinted down the path that curved this way and that through the center of the park. Though nobody else was in sight anywhere, they were confident that somewhere they would find their friend. And as they approached the drinking fountain, she suddenly came around a bend in the path ahead of them.

Preoccupied though they were with their own problems, Mrs. Graymalkin's appearance on that memorable occasion was enough to sweep thoughts of everything else out of their minds.

They were used to seeing her in her black cape worn over a black dress. Her customary hat, too, was a large black one with an enormous black feather trailing from it, a feather that looked as if it had been plucked from the tail of some peacock who was in mourning.

Tonight, however, she was transformed. She was dressed from head to foot in scarlet!

Even the high heels of her black shoes were red. Her huge and floppy scarlet hat was decorated with an extravagantly

24

long scarlet plume that quivered with every toss of her head. Her cape and her dress were both scarlet, trimmed with gold rickrack, a sort of zigzag braid.

"Mrs. Graymalkin!" cried Kerby, and could say no more. He was dazzled by such unexpected magnificence.

"Why, it's Kerby! And Fenton!" Mrs. Graymalkin treated them to an arch smile that displayed several large teeth, and about the same number of equally large gaps between them. "How nice to meet you dear boys on this night of nights, this special evening, when I'm all dressed up for a party!"

Fenton managed to speak.

"Good evening, Mrs. Graymalkin."

"Mrs. Graymalkin, indeed! Tonight I'm Mrs. Redmalkin!" she said, having her little joke. "How do you like my party clothes?"

Her cape whirled out in a wavy circle and her plume swung like a weather vane in a storm as she spun around in front of them. The effect was scintillating, coruscating, and downright pyrotechnical. In the dusky light, the gold trim seemed to give off sparks.

"You look terrific!" cried Kerby. "Doesn't she, Fenton?"

"You certainly do, Mrs. Graymalkin," said Fenton. "I'm glad we had to find you."

"You had to find me? And why did you have to find me, pray tell? Here it is Halloween, I'd think you'd be busy getting ready to creep out into the night and play some lively pranks on that lady with the cat who lives next door to you."

"How did you know?" marveled Kerby.

"I just had a feeling," said Mrs. Graymalkin.

"Well, you're right. We *were* getting ready to do that, until my cousin Gay had to go and do what she did."

"Gay? Gay? What a nice name!"

"We need help," said Kerby, sticking to the subject. "We're in an awful mess!"

"Not again? Kerby, it does seem to me —"

"But this wasn't our fault! It's that darn cousin of mine!"

"You mean Gay? And what has dear little Gay done? With a name like that, I can't imagine her being a troublemaker."

"You don't know Gay!"

"I see, I see. Well, tell me what happened."

Kerby told her. When he had explained the situation, he said, "And now we're afraid she'll slip up and say something, and my mother will find out about the chemistry set you gave me, and then . . . and then . . ."

As Mrs. Graymalkin stood looking down at him with her shrewd old eyes twinkling more and more amid the cobweb net of wrinkles that covered her face, Kerby's words trailed off and he hung his head. But then he looked up again.

"Well, you know how parents are," he said.

"Yes, yes, I know, I know," said Mrs. Graymalkin with a

droll croak that would have sounded completely at home in a crow's nest. "We do have to think of that. They might not understand. And we wouldn't want them to worry about anything, would we?"

"We certainly wouldn't!"

"Well, well, well. And what do you propose to do about all this?"

"Well, Fenton has an idea. Tell her about it."

Fenton obliged. Mrs. Graymalkin listened intently, and looked pleased with him. She nodded so vigorously that the scarlet plume on her hat swooped down and tickled the end of Kerby's nose.

"Good thinking, Fenton," she said, "good thinking. Very scientific, too, and I know how fond you are of science," she added with a sly cackle. "Hypnotism is becoming quite a modern technique in the treatment of many disorders."

"That's right. The only trouble is, we don't know how to hypnotize her," said Fenton, "so can you tell us how?"

Rolling up her eyes in an attitude of powerful concentration, Mrs. Graymalkin laid one long bony finger alongside her long bony nose. There was something about that finger, placed just so, bone to bone, that always seemed to stimulate her thoughts. Watching her, Kerby felt their troubles were over. He had great faith in Mrs. Graymalkin's thinking finger.

28

"Yes, indeed, now let me see. Perhaps the simplest approach would be to . . . Yes, I think that will do nicely . . ."

The think session was over. She removed the finger from alongside her nose, and nodded.

"Since Gay wants to see a magic trick done with your chemistry set, we might as well make use of it," she said. "Now, listen carefully. . . ."

Throwing her head back, she chanted solemnly.

"From four from right and two from left take two from right and four from left!"

Then she looked down at them again.

"Is that clear?"

Now it was Fenton's turn. He pondered deeply, so deeply that beads of perspiration appeared on his high forehead. This was Fenton's department. Kerby let him take full charge of it. And after a moment, Fenton came through.

"From the fourth tube from the right, and the second from the left, take two drops from the right and four drops from the left," he said.

Mrs. Graymalkin beamed, and patted him on the head.

"Fenton, you're becoming an absolute expert," she declared. "That's perfectly correct. Put the drops together in a beaker. Add about an ounce of water. Oh, we could go through a lot of fiddle-faddle about so many cubic centimeters of water, but an ounce, more or less, will do quite as well. Add the water. Stir carefully until the mixture begins to bubble and smoke. Dear little Gay will enjoy that part, and we may as well let her have some fun before she forgets all about what has happened. Once the mixture is bubbling and smoking well, hand her the beaker and tell her to sniff it. When she does, she'll want to drink it. What is more, she *will* drink it."

Kerby felt a twinge of anxiety.

"Sounds almost like that lemonade trick you had me do when you first gave me the chemistry set," he said. "Are you sure this won't work the way that did?

"Oh, my, yes. Never fear, Kerby, never fear. This will merely cause her to be hypnotized. Then you must tell her to forget all about the chemistry set and magic tricks and your friend Mrs. Graymalkin. Next, put your chemistry set away safely in its place, and lead her upstairs. When you are upstairs, say, 'Awake, Cousin Gay!' three times. The third time she will awake as though nothing had happened, and you can go on about your business with poor Mrs. Pembroke — do I remember her name correctly?"

"That's right. Gee, you're a great help, Mrs. Graymalkin!" Kerby felt as if a huge weight had rolled off his shoulders. "As soon as my mother and Aunt Martha leave, we'll do the trick."

"Good, good, good. And now I must hurry on, because I want to take a good long constitutional this evening, so as to be in tip-top shape for the party. Have a good time tonight, boys, don't eat too much trick-or-treat candy!"

With a final cackle Mrs. Graymalkin teetered away swiftly on her splendid red high heels and disappeared down the path. For an old lady she could really get a move on when she wanted to, but even so it seemed as if she whisked herself out of sight even more quickly than usual. All at once the boys realized why it seemed so.

"Hey, what do you know?" said Kerby. "It's getting foggy!"

In its strange and silent way, fog was beginning to roll in and settle under the trees, turning them into misty gray ghosts.

"A foggy night for Halloween!" said Fenton. "Who could ask for anything better than that?"

"Come on," said Kerby, "let's go home before we're in trouble. As soon as Mom and Aunt Martha leave, we'll take care of Gay — and then we'll take care of Mrs. Pembroke!"

As they jogged up through the park, enjoying the spooky effects of the fog, Kerby was able to think about an interesting matter there had been no time to consider before.

"I wonder what kind of party Mrs. Graymalkin is going to? It's funny she picked tonight of all nights to make such a big fuss about."

"Now, don't start imagining things," said Fenton, instantly on guard. "It's probably only a card party, or something like that."

"Maybe so," said Kerby, "but I wish we knew."

When they reached home, their supper was ready. Three places were set at the kitchen table. Already sitting at one of them was a small Halloween witch, complete in every detail. Below a tall, pointed black hat with a round brim, a mask with a long crooked nose and a scraggly-toothed grin leered at them. A long black gown completed the effect. Gay had her costume on and was ready for action.

"Hey, that's a pretty neat outfit," Kerby admitted.

Gay pulled off her mask.

"You've been gone a long time," she complained.

"Never mind, everything's all set."

"What's this all about?" asked Kerby's mother.

"Halloween stuff," he replied.

"Secrets, eh?" said Aunt Martha. "Well, have fun. I know Gay will. She's really been looking forward to this evening. But do be careful crossing streets in this fog."

"We will, Aunt Martha."

Next Kerby's mother issued a few orders.

"Now, I want you to come home not later than nine o'clock. We'll be back by then, and Aunt Martha will want to take Gay home. So nine o'clock, and I don't mean nine-oh-one. You see to it your Aunt Martha isn't sitting here worrying about Gay."

"Okay, Mom."

"And another thing," she added. "I don't want to have to listen to any complaints from Mrs. Pembroke tomorrow."

"Don't worry, Mom, you won't," said Kerby confidently.

"I'd better not. Sit down, now, so we can feed you. There's no dessert — you'll get plenty of that trick-or-treating!"

A few minutes later Kerby's mother and Aunt Martha had gone and they were alone, and safe at last. As Kerby relaxed, he decided it was only fair to give credit where credit was due.

"I'm glad you didn't blab anything, Gay."

"I kept still all the time, but it wasn't easy. I could hardly wait for you to come back. Did you see Mrs. Graymalkin?"

"Yes."

"And she told you how to do a trick?"

"Yes."

"Oh, good! When are you going to do it?"

"As soon as we finish eating."

Fenton had consumed his first hamburger and was about to start on his second. But now he put it down. He was looking thoughtful again.

34

"Why don't we do the trick now, and then come back and finish eating?" he said. "It won't take long."

At first Kerby was surprised by this suggestion. What was all the rush about? They had hardly started to eat. He for one was still hungry. But then the soundness of Fenton's thinking dawned on him. If they did the trick now, and brought Gay back to the table afterwards, they'd all be sitting there eating when he said, "Awake, Cousin Gay!" three times and she snapped out of it. It would seem very natural to her to be sitting at the table.

He tried not to grin at his brilliant friend as he pushed his chair back.

"Fenton, that's a great idea!" said Kerby. "Let's go downstairs."

"Oh, good!" cried Gay. "I'm so excited I can hardly eat anyway!"

4

IN A CORNER beside the table, Waldo was also dining. He was a fast eater, however. His food dish was almost empty. When they left the table to go downstairs, he took a last quick bite or two, licked his chops, and padded along behind them.

Though no longer a puppy, Waldo was far from large. A shaggy coat of long hair filled him out into something sizable enough to pass for a dog, however, and enabled him at least to look larger than Xerxes, the cat next door.

Waldo watched with interest now as Kerby opened the toy chest and took out the long wooden box he kept in it. Waldo had seen that box many times before. He knew it had something to do with his friend Mrs. Graymalkin, whom he had met so often with Kerby over in the park, and whose interesting old car he had ridden in on a couple of occasions. He even knew that some odd things had happened in connection with that long wooden box. But since he had a dog's normally short memory about some matters, he could not recall exactly what had taken place.

Kerby carried the chemistry set to the workbench and

opened it up. On the inside of the lid, in faded red and black letters, appeared the words:

FEATS O' MAGIC CHEMISTRY SET
Instructive! Entertaining!
Hours of Amusement!
Astonish Your Friends!
Entertain at Parties!
Make Extra Money Giving Demonstrations!

Slowly, stumbling over some of the big words, Gay read it all aloud.

"Gee, Kerby, could you really Make Extra Money Giving Demonstrations?" she asked eagerly.

"Well, yes, I probably could," said Kerby, remembering some of the spectacular private demonstrations he had given without necessarily intending to, "but I wouldn't want to try."

"Why not?"

Kerby grinned at Fenton.

"Well, as Fenton says, Mrs. Graymalkin is a little ahead of her times. I don't think most people are ready for her tricks yet."

"I don't understand," said Gay.

"Never mind," said Kerby, "just watch."

He handed Fenton a glass tube with markings on its side.

"One ounce of water, please, O Faithful Helper."

"At once, O Wise One," said Fenton with a low bow. He took the tube to the basement sink and filled it to the thirty-cubic-centimeter level, which he knew was about an ounce.

Kerby inspected the chemistry set. Because of past experiments, there were several gaps in the row of tubes containing chemicals. But there were still plenty left. He rubbed his hands together. "Now, then! Together, O Faithful Helper, let us chant the magic formula."

His assistant bowed again, and cleared his throat impressively.

"From four from right and two from left take two from right and four from left," they chanted in unison. Neither of them got a single word wrong. They were always careful to remember Mrs. Graymalkin's instructions exactly. A lot depended on that.

Starting from the right side, Kerby counted tubes.

"One, two, three, four. The fourth tube from the right."

Uncorking the tube, he took an eyedropper and a small glass beaker from the compartment that held the apparatus. He set the beaker on the workbench.

"How many drops, O Faithful Helper?"

"Two drops, O Wise One."

"You are correct."

Using the eyedropper, Kerby let two drops fall into the

beaker. He corked the tube and returned it to its place. Next he picked out the second tube from the left.

"How many drops from the second tube from the left, O Faithful Helper?"

"Four drops, O Wise One."

"Again, you are correct. Remind me to reward you with a handful of priceless jewels when I have finished."

Using a second eyedropper, Kerby let four drops fall into the beaker. Then he raised it in both hands and turned.

"Now stand before us, O Princess of the Night, at three paces distance, and marvel," he commanded.

Bursting with excitement, but quick to do her part, Gay took her place in front of him and turned away. Her black gown rustled as she took three big steps, counting them as she did so, "One, two — three!" This done, she turned and faced them. It was all Kerby could do not to spoil the great moment by laughing. In her tall pointed black hat and long black gown, Gay looked like the smallest and merriest witch that ever climbed on a broomstick.

Sitting on the floor next to Kerby, Waldo was watching everything with an indulgent eye. He always enjoyed a silly good time. He started to get up and join Gay, but Kerby said, "No, O Four-Footed Friend, remain here with the magicians. . . . Waldo! That means you! Sit down!" So Waldo sat down again beside his master.

With a flourish, Kerby waved one hand toward Fenton.

"Pour in the water, O Faithful Helper!"

Fenton made another low bow. They exchanged an excited look and a quick grin, and then Fenton poured the water into the beaker.

POO-O-O-O-OOF!

A heavy, foggy mist erupted from the beaker and rolled above their heads. Like a thick cloud it settled around Kerby and Fenton and Waldo. For a moment they couldn't see a thing, and Gay couldn't see them. Then, just when she thought they had disappeared for good, and was about to be really scared, the mist cleared away.

Gay burst into delighted laughter. She clapped her hands and danced with glee.

"Oh, Kerby, that was wonderful! You look so f-funny!" she cried, and bent double with a fit of the giggles.

Kerby stared at the beaker in his hands. There was nothing left in it, not a drop. How could they hypnotize her, if there was nothing left for her to drink? Something had gone wrong. Kerby turned to Fenton to remark about it.

He never got the words out of his mouth. Instead, he simply goggled. And Fenton goggled back at him.

"F-Fenton!" stammered Kerby. "Where did you get that mustache?"

Fenton's long solemn face was adorned by a big fierce black mustache with curling ends. His hand darted to it and felt it. His mouth fell open under it.

"A mustache! And where did you get that beard?"

Kerby clapped his hand to his chin. He felt crisp, curling hair.

"You look like Abraham Lincoln!" cried Gay, still whooping with laughter. "Oh, that's the funniest trick I ever saw!"

With one accord the boys rushed to a small mirror that was hanging over the sink, and shoved against each other trying to get a glimpse of their faces.

Kerby groaned. "I *do* look like Abraham Lincoln!"

Fenton moaned. "And I look like a movie villain!"

"Let me have your beard, Kerby," said Gay. "I want to try it on."

"What do you mean, try it on?" snapped Kerby. He gave it a tug that hurt. "It's *there!* It's real!"

Fenton pulled at his mustache.

"Ow! So's mine!"

Waldo had sprung up and was watching them with a dumbfounded expression. Now, suddenly, he shivered. The basement seemed to have become drafty. He was so amazed at the way Kerby and Fenton looked, however, that he didn't pay much attention to a little thing like that. Then his side

42

tickled, and he sat down absentmindedly to scratch with his hind foot.

"Yipe!"

Waldo jumped as though a bee had stung him. That was how his sharp nails felt against his hide. His yelp of pain made the others glance around at him.

"Cripes! Look at Waldo!"

From his shoulders all the way back to his tail, Waldo looked as if he had been shaved. All his long shaggy fur was gone, except for a little fluff around each ankle and a little fluff on the tip of his tail.

"Why, he looks just like a poodle!" cried Kerby, but he was wrong. Not being a poodle, Waldo did not look just like a poodle at all. Instead, he looked like a small shaggy dog who was *trying* to look like a poodle and making a bad job of it. When poodles are trimmed in poodle fashion they look funny and yet they look all right. But on Waldo a poodle trim looked ridiculous.

After letting out his howl, he peered around sharply to see what had made his claws sting him. When he saw his bare side, the hair that was still left on his head and shoulders stood straight up. He turned and looked at his other side. Then he looked down at his legs. Then he looked back at his tail.

Then he sat down and howled in earnest.

"OOO-ROO-ROO-O-O-O!" howled Waldo, and a more pitiful sound never issued from dog's lips since the beginning of time. With his big orange-and-black bow still around his neck, he was a tragic figure.

Springing to his feet, Waldo made for the stairs. Followed by his friends, he rushed up to the kitchen, through the house to the living room, and up the stairs to the second floor. He kept going till he reached a bathroom where there was a full-length mirror he could see himself in. When he got there, he took a good look.

Then he threw his head back and really outdid himself.

"OOO-ROO-ROO-ROO-O-O-O-O!" howled Waldo, all the way up the scale and down again.

For one thing, he happened to know a couple of poodles in the next block, and the last thing he wanted to do was look like them. For another thing, without his fur he looked no larger than a puppy again.

Waldo had endured some bad moments in his time, but this was his grimmest hour.

In the meantime, Gay had stopped laughing. She was not laughing at all now. She was indignant. She even burst into angry tears.

"Kerby, your beard is funny, but *that's* not funny!" she wailed, pointing a quivering finger at Waldo. "That's *mean!*"

5

GAY stamped her foot angrily.

"You change Waldo back this *minute*," she ordered, "or I'll tell Aunt Pris everything!"

Kerby had heard hollow threats before, but this was the hollowest. He greeted it with a suitably hollow laugh.

"If we don't get him changed back, you won't have to tell her. Stop acting so dumb! You don't think we did all this on purpose, do you?"

Gay stopped crying and stared at him.

"But you did a trick —"

"Yes, but something went wrong! This wasn't the way the trick was supposed to work."

Gay blinked.

"It wasn't?"

"No, it wasn't! And now I've got a real beard and Fenton's got a real mustache and we're in a real mess!"

He eyed Waldo's condition.

"Hey! Do you think . . . ?"

Fenton tested the texture of his mustache between thumb and forefinger.

"No. It doesn't *feel* like dog fur."

"Then why . . . ?"

"Beats me. I guess the stuff in the beaker must have a different effect on animals. Sort of an opposite effect."

Kerby examined himself again in the bathroom mirror and tugged unhappily at his new adornment.

"If this is Mrs. Graymalkin's idea of a funny Halloween trick, all I can say is —"

"I can't believe she'd do this to us," said Fenton, twirling his mustache thoughtfully. "There must be some other explan —"

He stopped in the middle of a word. Slowly, as a dreadful possibility occurred to him, he directed a terrible gaze down at Gay.

"Gay! When you were looking at the chemistry set, did you touch any of the tubes?"

First her eyes widened. Next they became shifty. As she looked around, she looked everywhere except at Fenton or Kerby.

"Well, yes, I did — but only one. Or maybe two. Two at the very most."

"What did you do with them?"

"I just looked at them. I didn't take the corks out or anything. I wanted to smell them, but I didn't have time, because I heard you coming."

"What did you do with them then?"

"I put them back in the box."

"In exactly the same slots you took them from?"

Gay fidgeted.

"Well . . ."

"You didn't!"

"Well, you made me hurry! I was trying to hide the magic set fast, so I put them back quick and I'm not sure whether . . . whether . . ."

Her voice trailed off as they all realized what had happened.

"So it wasn't Mrs. Graymalkin's fault at all," Fenton pointed out with a certain gloomy satisfaction.

"Gay mixed up the tubes," said Kerby, "and we got the wrong combination."

His little cousin looked up at them forlornly.

"But I didn't *mean* to —"

"No, you never mean to," snapped Kerby, pulling his beard angrily, "but you always manage to mess things up just as bad as if you did! Why don't you ever learn to mind your own business, anyway? Now look at the mess you've got me into! I've got to shave this thing off!"

"That wouldn't do any good," Fenton pointed out. "It would still show. You know how your father looks. Even with a fresh shave, you can still see his whiskers. Besides, I've got a better idea — and there's no time to lose! Come on!"

"Where are you going?"

Fenton paused at the door, his mustache bristling with excitement.

"Mrs. Graymalkin is the only one who can help us now. We've got to find her before she leaves the park!"

"You're right," said Kerby, "but wait a minute! We can't go running out in the street looking the way we do, with beards and mustaches!"

"Oh, that's true," said Fenton. But then he had another thought. "Still, why not? It's Halloween!"

"Hmm. You've got something there. But still . . . That mustache of yours looks so real it's scary. If anyone sees us who knows us, they might get curious and — Listen, I know! I've got some old masks we can wear. You know, that pirate mask, and the skeleton one . . ."

All four of them hurried down the hall to Kerby's room. He produced the masks from a box in his closet.

"Let me have the pirate one," said Fenton. "That will go best with my mustache."

The mask only came down over the cheeks, with a straggly mustache dangling from the bottom of it.

"I certainly don't need *two* mustaches," said Fenton, and snipped off the false one with a pair of scissors from Kerby's desk. Then he tried on the mask in front of the mirror.

"There, now! How's that for a real pirate mustache?"

Kerby tried on his mask, and was less well satisfied. His beard bushed out below it.

"Who ever heard of a skeleton with a beard?" he grumbled.

"Don't worry, nobody will think anything about it."

"I hope not. Okay, now what about Waldo? He's got to go along."

The mere mention of this possibility made Waldo hide under the bed.

"Hey, come back here!" cried Kerby, dragging him out again.

"Listen, you know very well Waldo will never set foot out of the house looking like that," said Fenton. "Besides, he'd be cold. He's used to fur."

This time it was Gay who came up with an idea.

"Why can't he wear one of your sleeveless sweaters, Kerby?"

"What a crazy idea!" scoffed Kerby, but Fenton nodded.

"Maybe she's right, Kerby. Anyway, let's try it."

While Waldo backed into a corner, Kerby pulled open a drawer and located a sweater.

"Now, look, Waldo, you can get away with it all right because it's Halloween. Besides, it's foggy and hardly anyone will see you," Kerby pointed out as they surrounded him. With something like a sigh Waldo allowed them to drag the sweater over his head and pull his front legs through the armholes. Now his bow looked like a scarf around his neck.

"There, that's fine," said Fenton, "and anyway, we haven't got time to argue about it. Let's go!"

Waldo trotted down the hall to the bathroom for a look at himself, and what he saw made him roll his eyes in anguish. But at the same time he sensed that if ever he was to get his fur back, he had better stay with them. So when Kerby called he squared his shoulders, set his jaw, and followed the others downstairs.

"I nearly forgot *my* mask," said Gay. It was lying on the kitchen table. Kerby thought about its more than slight resemblance to their friend in the park.

"Never mind," he said.

"That's right," said Fenton. "Leave it here. You'll understand why when — when — Well, anyway, leave it here."

They slipped out the back door. Outside it was so dark and foggy that they had to grope their way down the steps from the back porch. With Kerby in the lead they picked their way single file around the house to the sidewalk. There the street lamps, yellow blobs of light in the fog, made the going easier.

But as luck would have it, another yellow blob was sitting on top of the terrace beside the steps that led up to Mrs. Pem-

broke's house. It was Xerxes, out for a breath of air and a prowl around before retiring for the night. And unfortunately the big cat got a good look at Waldo.

There is no use pretending that poor Waldo was at his best. For one thing, the sweater fit him snugly, making him seem quite small and insignificant. Furthermore, he simply was not the kind of dog who looked well in a sweater. And besides that, the sweater did nothing to hide his pipestem legs, with their bits of fluff at the ankles. Xerxes surveyed him from head to tail, and collapsed in a heap on the ground.

"MROW-HOW-HOW-HOW!"

Cats are not supposed to laugh. This is a known scientific fact. Nevertheless, the noise Xerxes made sounded suspiciously like cat laughter. The way he sprawled on his stomach in the grass and beat his front paws on the ground looked remarkably like someone enjoying a good joke.

Stung to the quick, Waldo bared his fangs and sprang up the terrace, expecting Xerxes to make his customary dash for the nearest tree. But Xerxes just lay there. He glanced up with an "Are you kidding?" expression and continued to shake his sides and beat on the ground with his paws.

Waldo was so mortified that his growl trailed off into a whimper. When Kerby said, "Come on! We haven't time for that!" he was only too glad of an excuse to slink away down the slope and leave Xerxes to his merriment. What was left of

Waldo's tail was between his legs. If ever a dog was broken in spirit, it was he.

The street seemed deserted, but not for long. Kerby and his group had not gone far when something ahead of them made them skid to a halt, gasping. A vague figure, tall and dim in the fog, was standing under one of the street lamps. It was wearing a black cape and a pointed black hat. It had a big bag hanging from one shoulder. Its hands held a clipboard and a pencil.

"Well!" said an oily voice, "hello, trick-or-treaters! Don't be afraid, I'm just a nice old wizard with a bag full of candy bars! I work for some nice people who make all kinds of Halloween costumes and other fun things, and we're doing a survey of what you kiddies wear on Halloween. All you have to do is answer a few simple questions and you'll each get a great big chocolate candy bar from my bag of goodies!"

Fenton was the first to recover from his fright and find his voice.

"Well, I'm sorry, but we're in a hurry —"

"Won't take a minute," said the man, writing busily on his clipboard. He peered down at them, and then, before Fenton could stop him, plucked off Fenton's mask and examined it eagerly. "Say, this looks like one of ours! It is! Oh, dandy! Now, where did you buy this, sonny? Why, the mustache has been cut off! Where did you get the one you're wearing? By George, that's a good one!"

"It was given to me," said Fenton. "Please, let me have my mask back —"

"Just a few questions, and it's all yours," said the pest, holding it out of reach. "Just let me have a look at that mustache, and —"

In desperation Kerby bent down to Waldo.

"Sic 'em!" he whispered.

In his present frame of mind, nothing could have been more welcome to Waldo than a chance to express his feelings. Growling fiercely, he sprang forward, seized the man's trouser cuff, and began to worry it like an old washcloth.

"Hey!"

With a wild cry, the man sprang into the air, and when he came down he stumbled off the edge of the curb. Suddenly the air was full of sheets of paper and candy bars. Fenton made a grab for his mask and caught it in midair, and then he and the others were off down the street on a dead run, while behind them the oily voice had lost all its oil and become quite gritty.

"You little monsters! Now look what you've done!"

They did not stop to look. Instead they ran on to the corner as fast as they could.

"Darn him, anyway!" said Kerby. "If he makes us miss Mrs. Graymalkin —!"

It was very dark now, so dark that his heart sank into his shoes. Surely she would be gone. And if she was, what would they do? They might as well keep right on running. How could they ever go home now and face their parents — him with Abe Lincoln chin whiskers, Fenton with a huge mustache, and Waldo looking like an imitation poodle?

Across the street, a small red dot glowed feebly in the fog. Kerby's heart made a great leap, more or less back into its normal position.

"Look! I think that's Nostradamus's taillight!"

"Hurry!" cried Fenton. "I hear his motor running!"

6

AS THEY RACED across the street, the ancient sedan shimmied like a duck shaking himself after a swim. For Nostradamus this was normal procedure, merely a part of the business of getting under way. Bucking like a bronco leaving the gate at a rodeo, Nostradamus leaped forward.

"Mrs. Graymalkin! Wait!" cried Kerby.

Brakes squealing in protest, Nostradamus slowed down, coughed disgustedly, and stopped. The driver put her head out of the window and looked back.

"Kerby, dear! Is that you?"

"Yes!"

"Well, well! What's the matter now?"

"Something went wrong! We're in awful trouble!"

"Not again? Trouble, trouble! Lackaday!"

She opened the door and climbed down from the driver's seat.

"Well, children! Come, let's get out of the street, so we can talk safely."

She led the way to a grassy spot under a street lamp, where she could see them better. When Gay could see *her* better, she gasped with amazement — and said the right thing.

"Oh, what a beautiful dress!"

"Do you like it? It is lovely, isn't it? I had it made specially, and I do think it suits me. You must be little Gay, whom Kerby told me about," said Mrs. Graymalkin, looking pleased with her. "I might have known he'd have a nice little cousin like you."

"Wait till you hear what she's done *now,* you won't think she's so nice!" said Kerby bitterly.

"Now, now, don't tell me Gay has done something dreadful. I'm sure she didn't mean to. Fenton! Is that you?" said Mrs. Graymalkin, noticing him for the first time. "I would hardly have known you with that fine fierce mustache. And what is this?" she added, peering down at the animated sweater that was trying to hide behind everybody's legs. "Good heavens! Is that dear little Waldo?"

The whimper that escaped him at this point — flesh and blood can stand only just so much — made it clear she had guessed right.

"Waldo, what happened to you? You do look so . . . so . . ." She struggled to hold back a titter, but was only partly successful. "Oh, dear, oh, dear, I don't mean to laugh, but if

58

that is intended to be a Halloween costume, it's certainly the funniest —"

At these words Waldo sat down and howled his heart out.

"That's no Halloween costume," explained Kerby, "he's wearing my sweater because he hasn't any fur left!"

Mrs. Graymalkin stopped tittering and began to look properly concerned.

"What? No fur left? Gracious, that *is* serious, very serious indeed! Do tell me what is going on here." She examined Kerby more closely. "That beard, now. Why are you wearing a beard with a skeleton's head? And where did you get such a good one? It almost looks . . ."

She gave it a little tug.

"Ow!"

"Kerby! You don't mean . . ."

"Yes, mam. It's real."

Mrs. Graymalkin took a deep breath that made her scarlet cape quiver and sent sparks showering in all directions from its gold rickrack trim.

"Mercy me! Take off your masks."

The boys obeyed. She twirled one end of Fenton's mustache, and fingered Kerby's beard again.

"They're real, all right. Lackaday! Well, do tell me all about it."

"Well," began Kerby, "you know that trick you told us to do for Gay . . ."

"Yes, yes," she said, with a quick glance at Gay, "obviously it didn't come off the way it was supposed to."

"It certainly didn't. And we did it exactly the way you said to, only what we didn't know was that when Gay was looking at my chemistry set, she took out a couple of the tubes. When she heard us coming, she put them back fast, and didn't get them back in the same places. So four from right and two from left didn't come out right."

"Good gracious! I see, I see!" Mrs. Graymalkin closed her eyes tightly as she concentrated. "Yes, yes, she must have taken tube number five from the right and put it in the empty number two slot, and moved number two from the left over into number six on that side. That way, four from right would be number three, and two from left would be number three from that side, and three and three — Oh, that would be a meddlesome combination indeed, a most mischievous combination! Oh, dear, this is grave, very grave! I must think!"

And think she did. While they waited tensely, Mrs. Graymalkin thought and thought.

But to no avail!

For once the mighty thinking finger was laid alongside the long bony nose in vain.

Though she rolled her eyes, squinted, breathed deeply, and even scowled, the results were obviously disappointing. After a while she sighed sharply and spoke words Kerby had never expected to cross her lips.

"No, no, it's too difficult, simply too difficult. The complications are staggering. This is something I didn't foresee. . . ."

Kerby was thunderstruck. Mrs. Graymalkin stumped? Mrs. Graymalkin at a loss? His whole world seemed to be tumbling down around his ears. If *she* couldn't help them, then who could?

But then, just as his spirits reached their lowest ebb, Mrs. Graymalkin put her thinking finger back to work again.

"Hold on!" she said, rolling up her eyes for another try. "Maybe our answer doesn't lie with your Feats O' Magic set this time. . . ."

With a prodigious effort she squeezed her eyes shut and then popped them open again.

"That's it! It could be a matter of body chemistry," she said. "Yes, indeed! I think it very well might be. And if . . . Yes, yes, yes, that might do it."

She squinted down at them, and if a rapt audience is what she wanted, she achieved her desire. Few audiences have ever been rapter. Kerby was holding his breath. Fenton, obviously pleased with the scientific turn her remarks had taken, was hanging on her every word. Waldo's pathetically hairless tail was wagging like mad. Gay was poised on tiptoe.

"What your body chemistry needs is a sudden shock," declared Mrs. Graymalkin. "That might be just the thing to put matters right. What you three must have is a good scare."

Kerby goggled up at her.

"A good scare?"

"That's right. A real hair-raiser," she said, and then corrected herself. "Well, a hair-raiser in Waldo's case, that is, and a hair-ridder in yours and Fenton's. Now the question is, how are we going to get you a good scare?"

Kerby glanced around them into the fog, where every tree trunk looked as if it were wearing a shroud, where every terror of the night had ideal cover to slither around in, and despite all his worries he had to laugh. It was a small, feeble laugh, to be sure, but a laugh.

"Well, we've certainly got the right night for it," he said. "And Halloween besides!"

"Nothing to it," agreed Fenton. His voice throbbed with relief. "Let's see, now, what's the scariest thing we can do . . . ?"

"How about walking up to Indian Rock?" cried Kerby.

"Good idea!"

"Do you mean that large rock ledge at the far end of the park?" asked Mrs. Graymalkin.

"That's right," said Kerby. "Now, there's a place I stay away from after dark even on *summer* nights!"

"So do I," said Fenton. "I don't really believe those stories about how the Indians used to sacrifice their victims on top of it, but just the same it's a very sinister place. There's something about it that always gives me the shivers."

"It makes *me* shiver just to think about it!" Kerby declared enthusiastically. "If I didn't have a beard to get rid of, you couldn't drag me within a mile of the place! Here, Gay, you hang onto our masks — we won't need them now. Come on, Fenton, let's get it over with!"

"Go ahead, boys, and take Waldo with you," said Mrs. Graymalkin. "Gay and I will wait in the car."

"I wish I could go, too," said Gay enviously.

"You don't need a scare," said Kerby. "It would just be wasted on you."

"He's right, dear," said Mrs. Graymalkin. "You come along with me."

The boys peered down the slope at the gray-white fog that swirled slowly and silently under the trees, thinning out in places now, but only enough to make the trees seem more than ever like a gathering of waiting ghosts.

"Boy, is this creepy!" gloated Kerby. "Our worries are over. Let's go!"

7

SLOWLY, CAREFULLY they picked their way through the woods that grew thicker and thicker as they approached the far end of the park. They were deliberately traveling through the densest parts of the woods, instead of staying on the paths. More than once they stumbled over roots that writhed like snakes beneath their feet. Low branches clawed their cheeks like clammy, bony fingers.

"Gee, if anybody had ever told me I'd go near Indian Rock on Halloween, I'd have said they were crazy," muttered Kerby in a hushed voice. "I'm glad I'm afraid of the dark. It won't take much to scare *me,* let me tell you. Any little thing now, and I'll jump right out of my skin."

"Just jump out of your beard, that's all," said Fenton, and they both snickered. But then Kerby was angry.

"Hey, cut that out, Fenton! This is no time for making funny cracks. We've got to be serious!"

"You're right," agreed Fenton. He sounded sorry, and hastened to reassure his friend. "Don't worry, I only said that to sound brave. Actually, I'm scared to death."

"If you have to talk about something," said Kerby, forgetting that he was the one who had started the conversation, "then let's talk about human sacrifices and evil spirits and stuff like that. Maybe the Indians really *did* kill their victims on top of the rock."

"It's possible," said Fenton.

"Can't you just see them holding down an enemy brave and lifting up their tomahawks . . . ?"

"It must have been horrible," Fenton agreed helpfully.

"Then they would cut out his heart and hold it up dripping with blood . . ."

"That was the Aztecs," said Fenton.

"All right, maybe they just hit him on the head!" snapped Kerby, annoyed by the interruption. "But anyway, think of all the horrible things that may have happened in these very woods, and . . ."

Kerby stopped in his tracks and grabbed Fenton's arm in the dark.

"F-Fenton!"

"What is it? Did you see something?" asked Fenton hopefully.

"No, I just thought of something!"

"What?"

"We didn't put away the chemistry set!"

"Oh!"

66

"It's spread out all over the place down in the basement!"

"Golly, that's right!"

"What'll we do? If my family should come home early, we're sunk! We'd better turn around and —"

"No, now, wait a minute, Kerby. If we don't get back to looking normal, it won't matter much, anyway. We'd better take a chance and let it go till we've had our scare and got straightened out. We should still be home in plenty of time. But even if we're not, it would be better to let them find the chemistry set than to have them see us with a beard and mustache, and Waldo looking the way he does."

Waldo stood up with his paws against Kerby's side and looked up at him earnestly. He was indicating that he couldn't agree with Fenton more. Kerby gave in.

"Okay, then, let's keep going, but let's hurry," he said anxiously. "Gosh, we left everything —"

WHO-O-O-O-O-O!

"— right on the workbench," continued Kerby, as a fearsome hoot made the air tremble from a treetop directly above their heads.

"I know," said Fenton, "but stop worrying about it. . . . Say, wasn't that an owl just then?"

"What?" said Kerby. "Oh. Yes, that was an owl, all right."

Then he was angry all over again as he realized what an opportunity they had missed.

"Why did I have to think about that old chemistry set?" he cried. "If I'd been paying attention, I'd be all fixed up by now. Any other time an owl would have scared me stiff!"

"Me, too," said Fenton sorrowfully. "We've got to keep our minds on our business."

"You said it," agreed Kerby. "No more talking, huh?"

"Okay."

For a moment Kerby stumbled along in silence, concentrating fiercely on the tree trunks that seemed to come and go like specters around them. He did his best to imagine murderous Indians and shrieking victims. What he wouldn't give for just one good bloodcurdling shriek! Or one evil spirit bathed in an unearthly light —

"Fenton!" he cried, stopping again.

"What now?"

"We even left the light on in the basement!"

Now it was Fenton's turn to be annoyed.

"There you go again! Besides, we didn't. I turned it off."

"What? Are you sure?"

"Yes! Well, almost, anyway. I do things like that automatically."

"Hmm. Well, let me see, now . . ." Kerby stopped to think, leaning on one hand against an outcropping of granite that loomed out of the fog beside him, huge and menacing.

"Maybe you're right at that. When we left the house it was dark outside. We would have noticed if the lights were shining out of the basement windows. So I guess you're right, at that."

Fenton glanced up at the bulge of granite beside them, and groaned quietly.

"Kerby."

"What?"

"Do you know where we are?"

"No, where?"

"Indian Rock. You're leaning on it."

"Oh, for Pete's sake! How did we get here already?" Kerby took a look around. "Hey, Fenton."

"What?"

"Are your knees knocking?"

"No. Are yours?"

"No, darn it."

Fenton groaned again.

"Well, we're here, so we might as well go all the way. Come on, let's climb up on top."

Pawing around in the dark, they clambered to the very top of the great rock and sat down. They sat in a heavy silence for a moment. Then Fenton said, "Listen, you want to know what my trouble is?"

"What?"

"I'm so scared I'm not going to be scared that I can't get scared."

"I feel the same way," admitted Kerby. "If you ask me, we're just wasting our time here."

Their voices sounded loud and strange in the hush of that dark and silent place, where normally they would not have dared to speak in more than a tremulous whisper.

"Well, we've got to get ourselves that scare somehow," said Fenton.

"That's all there is to it," agreed Kerby. "Let's go back and see if Mrs. Graymalkin can think of anything else."

Leaving behind the dread rock that had terrified generations of local boys, they started back through the woods, with Waldo trotting along gloomily behind. They had not gone far when a sepulchral sound reverberated through the trees.

WHO-O-O-O-O-O!

Fenton sighed.

"There's that owl again."

Then something small and black darted through the darkness. Squeaking horribly, the Thing all but brushed their faces with its furry wings.

"There goes a bat," remarked Kerby.

"Yes, I saw him," said Fenton, and they continued on their way, leaving behind a disappointed owl and a discouraged bat whose Halloween had been completely spoiled.

It was a dejected trio that approached Nostradamus a few minutes later.

"Well?" said Mrs. Graymalkin, when they came around the back of the car to her window. Gay, who was in the front seat with her, looked out at them, too. The car door was so high that Gay had to stand up inside and look over Mrs. Graymalkin's shoulder to see them.

"No luck," reported Kerby. "We just couldn't get scared."

When he told her about everything that had happened, Mrs. Graymalkin pursed her lips thoughtfully.

"Well, I'm not surprised. That rock is small potatoes, if you ask me," she said. "I never have believed those stories about the Indians myself. Well, well, well. I can see that we've got to stop fiddling around and go somewhere that's really frightening. But never fear. I know just the place. Jump in the back seat, boys."

Exchanging a hopeful glance, they climbed into the car with Waldo behind them. When they were all settled inside, Mrs. Graymalkin started the engine. At least, she tried to. Nostradamus wheezed and sneezed and snorted, but would not start.

"Nosy doesn't like this damp weather," said Mrs. Graymalkin. "It brings on his asthma."

Fenton fingered his mustache nervously, and glanced at his watch.

"Come on, Nosy!" he urged. "We only have till nine o'clock."

"That's right," said Kerby. "They're coming home by then, and we've got to be there!"

Mrs. Graymalkin tried again. This time the old car began to cough and sputter and clatter. Finally the engine started producing a variety of sounds that would have been a great help to a marimba band.

"That's the spirit! Just needed to clear his throat!" she declared, and away they went with the fenders flapping like buzzards' wings and the brass-rimmed headlights throwing fuzzy circles of light on the fog ahead of them.

Once he got going, Nostradamus really moved. The fog was so thick that Kerby lost all track of where they were. Naturally, on a night like that, there were hardly any other cars on the streets. Even so, he wondered how Mrs. Graymalkin could drive so fast in such thick fog without its being dangerous, until Fenton pointed out that she had her radar on. There was a radar screen on Nostradamus's dashboard which she had used when they were with her once before. By watching the radar, as she explained to Gay, they could tell whenever another car was anywhere near them. For such an old car, Nostradamus had many unusual features.

They drove on and on, while the minutes sped by and their nine o'clock deadline drew ever nearer. Kerby checked his watch and wished he hadn't. It was already eight o'clock! A horrible vision flashed into his mind before he could stop it, a vision of his mother looking at him for the first time. Until now he had only been worrying about himself. Suddenly he realized how awful it would be for her to discover that her son had become a little freak with chin whiskers. She would be heartbroken. She would cry. Anything, any disgrace or suffering or punishment, would be better than letting that happen. He *had* to get rid of his beard!

Mrs. Graymalkin slowed the car down and peered out of her window.

"I'm looking for street signs," she explained. "The one I want is not easy to find, especially on a night like this. . . . Ah, there it is!"

Kerby pressed his nose against the window beside him. Fenton leaned over to look, too. A third nose, wet and black, was pressed against the window below theirs. Under a street lamp, Kerby was barely able to read the sign. It was a strange, dim sign that looked transparent in the fog.

It read, BALD MOUNTAIN ROAD.

"This is it," said Mrs. Graymalkin, and turned sharply into a narrow lane that ran sharply uphill.

74

8

KERBY AND FENTON gaped at the sign, and then stared at each other. Their eyes carried on a silent argument. They could not very well argue out loud about what was on their minds, not when they were sitting in the car with Mrs. Graymalkin.

"I didn't know there were any mountains around here," Kerby remarked in a general sort of way.

"Oh, they only call it that," said Mrs. Graymalkin. "It's really no more than a big hill. The party I'm going to later on this evening is in this neighborhood, as it happens, but where we're going is on the very top."

"Oh."

Kerby thought for a moment. Then he cleared his throat.

"This party you're going to, Mrs. Graymalkin," he said. "Is it a card party?"

Her reply made him dig a triumphant elbow into Fenton's ribs.

"A card party? Oh, my, no," she said. "It's a dance."

Kerby was greatly encouraged by the effect Bald Mountain

Road and Mrs. Graymalkin's remarks were having on him. He was goose pimples from head to toe. To help matters along even more, they were tipped well back in their seats at an alarming angle, because Nostradamus seemed to be going almost straight up.

As they went higher, the fog thinned out enough so that they could see the sides of the road. They were on a narrow lane between two high stone walls. Then Nostradamus slowed down and stopped, and Kerby saw that the headlight beams were shining dimly on a towering pair of wrought iron gates.

"Jump out and push the gates open, boys," ordered Mrs. Graymalkin.

They watched each other gulp, but then they scrambled out and walked ahead to the gates. Waldo came along, too. The gates were tall and heavy, and when the boys pushed them open they screamed like lost souls in torment. Kerby and Fenton stood aside while Mrs. Graymalkin drove Nostradamus through the gates and stopped.

The sky was clear enough to allow a few feeble rays of moonlight to fall on the treeless knob of land that appeared to be the top of Bald Mountain. The ghastly light shone coldly on various tall, narrow marble buildings, grass-covered mounds, dismal monuments, and crazily tilted stone slabs. As they walked up alongside the car, Kerby suddenly realized where they were.

"My gosh, it's a c-cemetery!" he quavered.

"That's right, Kerby, dear! This is an old, old cemetery. It's not used any more. For new people, I mean," said Mrs. Graymalkin. "Actually, it's a very unusual cemetery. Everybody buried here was hanged for some horrible crime or other, except for a couple of murderers who were shot trying to escape, and one man who had his head chopped off in very mysterious circumstances."

"It s-sounds unusual," admitted Kerby, who was beginning to feel more and more as if they were on the road to success.

"Now, I want you to walk up the hill . . ."

"You mean, we're going to w-walk through the cemetery?"

"That's right," said Mrs. Graymalkin, "on your way to the haunted house."

"The huh-huh-haunted h-house?"

"Yes, indeed. Just over the brow of the hill, on the edge of the cemetery, in a patch of dark woods, you'll find a small house. More than a hundred years ago the man who lived there was found dead in his bed — all of him except his head, that is. That was *under* the bed. He's the man I was just speaking about. Ever since then, nobody has lived in the house . . . at least, not for long . . ."

"You mean, there's a gh-gh —?"

"Well, *something* made the people who tried to live there come running down the hill gibbering with fright in the middle of the night," said Mrs. Graymalkin. *"Something* made them refuse ever to go back there again."

For a moment there was silence, especially outside the car.

"Well? Are you ready, boys?"

Fenton gave his mustache a tug, as though to build up his courage.

"Yes!" he said. "I'm ready."

"Good. Kerby?"

Kerby looked around at the grisly scene and thought about how nice it would be to get rid of his beard. Nothing less would have induced him to stir a single step farther into such a place.

"Okay, Fenton," he said. "L-let's go."

Mrs. Graymalkin gave them a cheery send-off.

"Maybe with luck," she said, "you won't get as far as the haunted house."

They walked away toward the top of the hill, following a path, weedy and overgrown, that led between two rows of gravestones. At first they walked so close together that from the car they must have looked like one fat boy with four legs. And even then, Waldo managed to stay between them.

"Just let one thing move," muttered Kerby, his eyes darting from a crumbling red brick crypt to a shadowy marble mausoleum, "just one thing, and it's good-by beard."

"I'm doing my best to believe that we might see something,"

said Fenton, "but you know how I feel about things like this. There's not one shred of scientific proof —"

Kerby was instantly exasperated.

"Oh, for crying out loud, Fenton! Listen, what more do you want? You saw that sign back there. BALD MOUNTAIN ROAD! And you heard her say she was coming back here later on for a party — a dance! And you remember the music we heard at that special concert, don't you — 'Night on Bald Mountain'?"

"Yes, I know, but —"

"The man said it was all about how the witches met on Bald Mountain on Halloween and danced till midnight! So what more do you want? How stubborn can you be?"

Fenton stopped. Folding his arms, he glared angrily at Kerby. Then he flung one hand out in a wide circle.

"Okay, go ahead. Show me a witch. Show me just one witch!"

Kerby glanced around them, scarcely knowing whether to hope or fear that he could meet Fenton's challenge. But nothing was in sight except tall gravestones tilted this way and that, and lugubrious funereal monuments, and silent tombs and crypts.

"It's too early," grumbled Kerby. "You heard what she said. The party doesn't start till later. And she didn't say it was going to be *here,* anyway."

80

Fenton frowned at him for a moment, and then snorted.

"Too early! Not here! Of all the feeble excuses I ever heard. . . ."

And with that he stalked away, walking on ahead. Kerby glowered at his thin, ramrod-straight back for a moment, and then followed him. Looking disgusted with the two of them, Waldo followed Kerby. For a dozen paces or so they all trudged along in grumpy silence. Then Fenton stopped once more.

"Now you've spoiled everything again!" he complained. "How can I get scared if you start arguing about witches? Listen, let's split up and go different ways, and then maybe we can get some results!"

"Suits me," snapped Kerby.

"You take that path and I'll take this one. I'll meet you by that big mausoleum on the ridge," said Fenton, pointing to a huge marble tomb that stood out lividly against the dark sky.

"Okay," said Kerby, and they stamped off in different directions. Waldo sat down to scratch himself gently through his sweater, and then trotted after Kerby.

Once they were alone, Kerby said, "All right, Waldo, start looking for cat ghosts, if you want to get your fur back." He peered around him at his nightmarish surroundings and did his best to recapture his goose pimple mood, but try as he might he could not work up any satisfactory terror. All he could think about was Fenton and his unshakable faith in science. Maybe Fenton was right, at that. It was very discouraging. He sat down on a tumbled marble slab and looked around to see if he could spot Fenton anywhere. As he did, he saw something move up near the big tomb. Something that swayed this way and that went shambling along among the gravestones and disappeared behind the mausoleum.

Kerby watched. He watched until it disappeared. Then he glanced down at Waldo.

"How do you like that?" he said, grinning. "Old Fenton's up there trying to give me a scare."

It was a nice, unselfish thing to do, and it made him feel ashamed that he had got into an argument with his friend about a silly thing like witches. On the other hand, maybe Fenton had picked a quarrel on purpose, to give him an excuse to suggest they split up, so that he could try to give Kerby a scare. It would be just like Fenton to help him get rid of his beard if he could, and help Waldo get his fur back, even if in doing so he didn't solve his own problem. For that matter, how could they ever get rid of Fenton's mustache? Fenton simply did not scare easily.

Still, if only they could get rid of his beard, thought Kerby, Fenton *could* shave off his mustache. It would hardly show, if he put on some powder afterwards. Maybe that was what Fenton had decided!

Jumping to his feet, Kerby hurried on up the hill to their meeting place. He was almost there when Fenton appeared around the side of the mausoleum. Kerby chuckled, and started to speak, but Fenton spoke first. He was also chuckling.

"I was looking for you," he said. "I saw you staggering around up here, trying to scare me."

Kerby stopped abruptly. The goose pimples were back.

"You wh-what?"

"I say, I saw you."

"But-but-but —"

"What's the matter?"

"But I saw *you!* I mean, I thought . . ."

Fenton stared at him. He knew Kerby well enough to know he wasn't fooling.

"You mean, that wasn't you?"

"No. Wasn't it you?"

"No!"

For a space of ten seconds they said nothing more. They were too busy looking around in every direction. A chill had started at the soles of Kerby's feet and was rapidly climbing up his back.

"Then who was it?" he wanted to know.

For once Fenton's face had a very unscientific pallor about it.

"M-maybe we're getting somewhere," he muttered. He twiddled his mustache with trembling fingers. "What was it we saw?"

"I don't know," said Kerby, "but it was Something!"

9

KERBY was as pale as the moonlight. Now, in an instant, everything was changed. Now they could stop trying to imagine things. Now Something was really there, somewhere in the dark, Something that could scare them to death. At last they were close to success. It did not take Kerby long to decide what to do next.

"I think I'll go back to the car," he said, and began to retreat briskly down the slope.

Fenton blinked. Then he ran after him.

"Hey, wait!" he cried, and grabbed him by the arm to stop him.

"Listen, I'm scared!" said Kerby. It was no time for false pride.

"Well, for Pete's sake, that's the *idea!*" said Fenton. "That's what we're here for, remember? You can't leave now, just when our big chance comes along!"

"Oh, can't I?" retorted Kerby. "Watch me. I'm as scared as I want to be right now."

Fenton eyed him sternly.

"You've still got your beard," he pointed out.

There was no doubt about that. Kerby's beard felt as if it were composed of ten thousand electric filaments. For that matter, the ends of Fenton's mustache were vibrating like the prongs of a tuning fork.

"I *know* I've still got my beard," said Kerby, scratching it with both hands. "It tickles like crazy!"

The itchy feeling was so bad that it helped stiffen his backbone. Even then he might not have gotten up nerve enough to turn around again if he had not thought once more of his mother, and his father, too. He glanced back up the slope at the grim mausoleum.

"Well," he said, "if you're game, I guess I am."

"Now you're talking," said Fenton. "We can't quit when we're this close. Come on!"

Silently Fenton led the way back toward the big tomb. It took all the courage they could muster to walk around the side of it, because that was where the shambling Something had gone out of sight. But nothing sprang at them from around the corner. They kept going. Silently Fenton pointed down the far slope of the hill toward some deep woods where Kerby could just make out the slant of a low roof. The haunted house. Silently, on legs that felt like tingling sticks, they walked toward it.

When they were near, they stopped and glanced at each

other. It was a small house, with low windows. It lay under the trees in deep shadows. It seemed to crouch there, waiting. A path led down through the trees to the side of the house. They took it. They ended up crawling on their bellies, until they were directly under a window.

The window had no glass left in it. They were about to raise up for a look when a surprise made them freeze.

From inside came a rasping sound, and a flare of light.

Somebody had struck a match.

A match? Ghosts didn't use matches. At least it didn't seem likely. Kerby felt Fenton nudge him. When he looked at him, Fenton jerked his head at the window. Kerby nodded. Carefully they raised up and peered in.

Four feet away, a small, untidy man was holding up a match and peering around him. As their heads came into view, he stared their way. He had small, bloodshot eyes. They became larger, much larger. The match shook so violently in his hand that it went out.

"Crikey! Midget ghosts!" he croaked. And with that he leaped for the door. In an instant he was gone. They could hear him yelling as he raced away down the hill.

Fenton sagged with disappointment.

"There goes our last hope!" mourned Kerby.

They exchanged a look of utter despair.

"Now what shall we do?"

"We might as well go back," said Fenton. "We've certainly used up *this* place!"

With whiskers drooping disconsolately, the boys and Waldo turned and walked away from the haunted house to the mausoleum on the crest of the hill.

"I'll never have any respect for Halloween again," said Kerby bitterly. "Of all the big fakes! Can't even give us one good scare!"

Fenton stopped to peer in through the wrought iron gates of the mausoleum.

"Nothing doing here," he reported in a deprived tone of voice, and rejoined Kerby and Waldo. Together they clattered down the hillside with a scornful disregard for all the queer shadows that came and went among the gravestones.

When they reached the car, Mrs. Graymalkin was peering out anxiously.

"Boys! What did you do to that poor man?"

"We scared *him,* instead of the other way around."

"Well, you certainly must have. I never saw a man run so fast. He ran straight out the gates, and I guess he's still running."

They made their report to her. When they had finished, she shook her head in a worried way.

"This is very discouraging," she said, "*very* discouraging. To think that my favorite cemetery would let me down this way."

She sighed heavily.

"Well, there's only one thing left to do," she said, and Kerby was glad to hear there was even one thing. But then she went on in a far from reassuring way. "I'd hoped it wouldn't come to this, because I'm not at all sure we can work out anything, but now we've no choice but to try."

Her old eyes flashed in the gloom.

"We'll simply have to fall back on your chemistry set, Kerby," she declared. "We'll go get it, and I'll see if there isn't *something* I can work out. I can't promise anything, but . . . we'll see . . ."

She drove Nostradamus outside, and together the boys closed the shrieking gates on their latest failure.

10

IT WAS A TENSE, miserable ride they had back down Bald Mountain and home along the foggy streets. Nostradamus went flying along, but so did the seconds and minutes.

Fenton consulted his watch grimly.

"Do you think we can make it home before nine o'clock, Mrs. Graymalkin?"

"It's going to be close," she admitted.

"Even if we do get the chemistry set, and even if you do work out something, we're still going to be in trouble now," Kerby pointed out unhappily. "By the time we finally get home, we'll be good and late."

With Kerby there was no question about whether or not he would be punished. When he had punishment coming, he got it. When his mother said nine o'clock, she meant business. And because of having Gay with him, and being responsible for her, it would go doubly hard with him if he was late. Any way he looked at it, with or without a beard, he was in for it. Unless . . . unless . . . There was one hope, and only one. If only his mother and Aunt Martha were late getting home themselves, then maybe —

"Here we are!" said Gay.

The fog had thinned out enough so that they could recognize the corner of Kerby's block as they turned into it. Kerby peered ahead eagerly, praying that he would see the house dark and —

"Duck!" he cried suddenly. "Duck, Gay! Keep going, Mrs. Graymalkin! That's Aunt Martha's car out front!"

"Yes, yes, I see it," said Mrs. Graymalkin. "Keep down. . . . Now we've passed them. Two nice-looking young women were sitting in it —"

"That's Mom and Aunt Martha!"

"They came back too soon!" complained Gay.

"Your house was dark, so they haven't gone in yet," added Mrs. Graymalkin. "I suppose they decided to sit in the car for a moment and watch for you to come home."

As Kerby had often found, one good thing about Fenton was that he never gave up. Even with disaster seconds away, his extraordinary brain continued to function. He well knew that all They had to do was get out of the car and go into the house and all was lost, yet even in the face of such immediate danger he still came up with a plan of action.

"Go around the block, Mrs. Graymalkin!" he cried. "We'll run across the vacant lot to the back door."

"Excellent, excellent," she agreed, and sent Nostradamus leaning around the corner, and the next corner as well, on two wheels. The old car skidded to a stop alongside the vacant lot.

"Now, Fenton, get out on my side of the car with Kerby," she ordered. "I want to tell you both exactly what to do. We can't afford any slip-ups at this point."

The boys scrambled out and stood beside her car door in an agony of eagerness to get going. Nostradamus was so tall that even Fenton's head barely came as high as the bottom of the window. The height made Mrs. Graymalkin seem very grand as she gazed down at them, like a judge on a bench.

"Now, then," she said. "Hold Waldo up to me, I want to feel his fur."

Almost driven frantic by the delay, but knowing that Mrs. Graymalkin must have some important reason for asking, Kerby lifted Waldo up. She reached down to feel the fur that was still around Waldo's head.

"Hmm. All right, you can put him down. Now, bring me only the four tubes closest to the right-hand side of the box. Repeat that, please."

"The four tubes closest to the right-hand side of the box!"

"Correct. Those are the only ones that may give us any help. And carry them carefully. You must keep cool heads, and take a chance that the ladies will stay in the car long enough to let you slip in and out again. Is that clear?"

94

"Yes!"

"Yes!"

"Then run!" said Mrs. Graymalkin, and they tore away like greyhounds across the vacant lot. Anyone else would have been in danger of taking a spill in the dark, but they knew every foot of the ground. They sped past their clubhouse, dim in the fog, and on to the fence. They were slipping through it when a familiar voice spoke in the milky darkness ahead of them.

"Xerxes!" it cooed in a low, coaxing tone. "Come here to Muvver, you naughty cat! You know you're supposed to stay in your very own yard!"

Now, Waldo had had a long and difficult night, full of vexations. To reach home again, then, only to find his personal back yard invaded by the champion smart aleck of the cat world was enough to make any self-respecting dog forget himself. Throwing caution to the winds, Waldo bared his teeth and rushed forward, barking his head off. Xerxes, who knew it was one thing to laugh in his own yard and another to linger in Waldo's, jumped four feet into the air with a yowl that could have been heard on Bald Mountain and streaked for home.

Because Mrs. Pembroke was stooping forward to peer through the thin place in the hedge, she received the full benefit of his passage through it. The last Kerby and Fenton saw of her was her big-eyed stare as she took in their bewhiskered

96

faces through the gloom, just before Xerxes sprang into her arms and sent her tumbling over backwards, screaming shrilly.

Nothing could have been less help to their cause.

By now They had surely heard Waldo's outburst, not to mention Xerxes's and Mrs. Pembroke's contributions. By now They were piling out of the car to find out what was going on. In a complete panic, with every hope gone, Kerby and Fenton sprang up the back steps followed by Waldo and burst into the dark house.

A flashlight blazed straight into their eyes!

"Yi-i-i!"

A burglar! Kerby was so scared he jumped back and fell over Waldo. In the front of the house a door opened, and lights went on. So did the kitchen lights. Before Kerby could do more than sit up, his mother hurried into the kitchen.

"What's going on here?"

Over by the light switch, Gay was dancing up and down.

"It worked!" she cried. "I pulled a trick on them, and it worked!"

Kerby's hand flew to his chin. His beard was gone!

As for Mrs. Maxwell, she was so relieved to find them unharmed that she was not angry.

"Well, you certainly gave us a scare!" she said.

Kerby stared unbelievingly at Gay.

"She gave *us* a scare!" he said. He felt his chin again and began to laugh wildly. "A *real* scare!"

His mother glanced at her watch.

"Nine on the dot. You really believe in shaving it close," she said, and her choice of words made him laugh even harder. "What was all that commotion in the back yard?"

"Waldo caught Xerxes in our yard and chased him out!" said Kerby, and noticed Waldo was nowhere in sight. Fenton, who was also sprawled on the floor, was fingering his smooth upper lip in a dazed way.

"Gay, I hope you didn't make a nuisance of yourself," said Aunt Martha.

"She was okay," said Kerby.

"Well, I'm glad to hear that. Did you have a good time, Gay?"

"Yes!"

"Get a lot of candy?"

"No, but who cares?"

"You mean, you played tricks on people instead?"

"You didn't pester Mrs. Pembroke, did you, Kerby?" his mother interrupted sternly.

"I should say not! It wasn't *our* fault Xerxes sneaked into our yard and bothered Waldo," he assured her, and glanced Fenton's way. Fenton was gone. Kerby sprang to his feet.

"Where is Waldo, anyway?" asked Mrs. Maxwell.

"Downstairs, I guess. I'll go see!" cried Kerby, and rushed down the basement steps. Gay followed him.

"Gay, we've got to go," her mother called after her.

"I'll be right back," called Gay, "I just want to say good-by to Waldo."

Fenton was already busy putting away the chemistry set. Waldo was hiding under the stairs. His sweater was all bulged out. Gay pulled it off over his head.

"Oh, Waldo, you look wonderful!"

Waldo thought so, too. Whining with joy, he whirled round and round in a circle to admire his bushy tail.

"Now you know why Mrs. Graymalkin told you to get out of the car on her side and hold up Waldo," said Gay. "That gave me a chance to sneak out of the car without any of you seeing me!"

She laughed merrily.

"She said there's nothing like a good scare right in your own house to *really* scare you!"

"I thought you were a burglar!" admitted Kerby.

"That's what you were supposed to think!"

While Gay was talking, they put away the chemistry set. Before they closed the toy chest, however, she produced a flashlight from under her black gown.

"She said to keep this, so you'd better hide it, too."

100

Fenton's face was glowing with scientific pleasure.

"Gay and a flashlight. Who could come up with a simpler trick than that?" he asked. "She's a master of psychology! A real master!"

"She's lovely!" said Gay. "She said I can be one of her friends from now on, too!"

Kerby suppressed a sigh. Hypnotism was obviously a lost cause.

"You won't tell anyone about her?"

"Of course not!"

They trooped upstairs and all went outside to the car when Aunt Martha and Gay were ready to leave. At that moment a familiar sight clattered past.

"There's that funny old car again," said Mrs. Maxwell. "It went by a few minutes ago."

Fortunately the children were behind her and Aunt Martha. Neither saw them wave. A curious cackling sound reached their ears, and then the ancient sedan disappeared into the fog.

Gay climbed into the car beside her mother and beamed out at the boys.

"I wish every Halloween could be as good as this one!" she said, and waved energetically as the car moved off. Kerby and Fenton exchanged a flabbergasted glance.

"Girls!" said Kerby, and he had never uttered the word with more feeling.